DATE DUE			

20752

E
W

Walton, Sherry.

Books are for
eating.

Books Are for Eating

BY **Sherry Walton**

PICTURES BY **Nadine Bernard Westcott**

E. P. DUTTON · NEW YORK

Here is our house.

This is Mama and me.... I'm Katy!

We have a baby, too.
His name is Alex.
Mama says I was like Alex once,
but I *couldn't* have been!

Know why? I'll show you.

We have lots of books in our house.
I know they're for reading.

But Alex thinks

books are for eating!

We have bunches of bananas in our house. I know they're for eating.

But Alex thinks

bananas are for squishing!

We have a cat named Butterscotch.
Her fur is for patting.

But Alex thinks

fur is for pulling!

We have a huge pile of clean diapers
every washday. I know what they're for.

But Alex thinks

diapers are for rolling in!

The drawers in our house
are for holding stuff.

But Alex thinks

drawers are for dumping!

We have lots of toys
to play with.

But Alex thinks

toys are for hiding!

This is Alex's playpen. It's for holding
him while Mama is upstairs.

But Alex thinks

the playpen is for
Butterscotch and Teddy!

We have a big sink in our bathroom.
I know the water is for washing.

But Alex thinks

it's for splashing!

Sometimes Mama lets us use straws.
I know they're for drinking.

But Alex thinks

straws are for blowing bubbles!

And so do I.
But don't tell Mama.

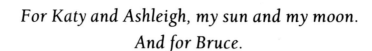

For Katy and Ashleigh, my sun and my moon.
And for Bruce.
Without them this book would not be.
S. W.

To my niece, Sarah.
N. B. W.

Published in the United States by E. P. Dutton,
a division of Penguin Books USA Inc.
Published simultaneously in Canada by
Fitzhenry & Whiteside Limited, Toronto
Designer: Martha Rago
Printed in Hong Kong by South China Printing Co.
First Edition   10 9 8 7 6 5 4 3 2 1

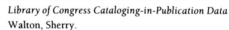

Library of Congress Cataloging-in-Publication Data
Walton, Sherry.
 Books are for eating.
 Summary: Little Katy is sure her own behavior as
a baby was never so appalling as her baby brother's—
well, most of the time, anyway.
 [1. Babies—Fiction.   2. Brothers and sisters—Fiction]
I. Westcott, Nadine Bernard, ill.   II. Title.
PZ7.W1776Bo   1989   [E]   89-11749
ISBN 0-525-44554-4